Silent Night

Silent Night

A Christmas Carol Is Born

by **Maureen Brett Hooper**

Illustrated by **Kasi Kubiak**

Boyds Mills Press

The publisher wishes to thank the Very Reverend Kevin P. Mulhern, Reverend Robert J. Simon, John Propeack, and Frank Williams for their assistance in developing this book.

Published by Caroline House
Boyds Mills Press, Inc.
A Highlights Company
815 Church Street
Honesdale, Pennsylvania 18431
Printed in China
Visit our website at: www.boydsmillspress.com

U.S. Cataloging-in-Publication Data
(Library of Congress Standards)

Hooper, Maureen Brett.
Silent night : a Christmas carol is born / by Maureen Brett Hooper ;
illustrated by Kasi Kubiak. — 1st ed.
[32] p. : col. ill. ; cm.
Summary: The story of how the Christmas carol "Silent Night" was created.
ISBN 1-56397-782-6
1. Gruber, Franz Xaver, 1787-1863. Stille Nacht, heilige Nacht — Juvenile
literature. 2. Gruber, Franz Xaver, 1787-1863 — Juvenile literature. Silent
night, holy night. 3. Carols, German — Texts — Juvenile literature. 4.
Christmas music — Texts — Juvenile literature. 5. Carols — Juvenile
literature. I. Kubiak, Kasi. II. Title.
782.28/1723 21 2001   CIP
00-112040

First edition, 2001
The text of this book is set in 16-point Goudy.

10 9 8 7 6 5 4 3 2 1

To Lawren and David
—M. B. H.

To Dan and Cindy,
and for the boys, Kyle and Tyler
—K. K.

Franz Gruber lit the candles on either side of the St. Nicholas Church organ. He slid along the bench until he sat before the keyboard. The organ pipes sparkled like a million jewels above him.

In the flicker of the candles, Franz studied the music. He could hear it in his head. He could feel it in his fingers. It was music written by Bach, a great composer.

"Tomorrow night we will have a wonderful Christmas Eve service," he thought.

Franz warmed his hands and prepared to practice.

A boy from the village school stood in his regular place behind the organ. He was there to work the bellows.

The boy stepped on the pedals and began to pump. Up and down went his feet. He forced the air into the organ pipes.

Franz began to play. But instead of the beautiful music that usually rose from the old organ, there came a terrible wheeze.

The boy held his ears.

Franz slipped from the organ bench to stand beside the boy. He studied the bellows. "They are leaking," he said. "The pipes can't make music. There's not enough air."

"Can't we repair them?" asked the boy.

"Not before tomorrow night," said Franz. He shook his head. "I was worried this would happen. The dampness from the spring flood has rotted the leather. These old bellows are beyond hope." Franz frowned. "I must tell Father Joseph we will not have organ music for the Christmas Eve service."

That night Franz paced the floor in his family's small living quarters above the schoolhouse where he taught. His children had gone to bed. The snore of the cat and the click of his wife's knitting needles were the only sounds in the room.

Mrs. Gruber stopped her knitting and studied the worried look on her husband's face. She wished she could help. "Is there anything we can do about the organ?" she asked.

"Nothing," replied Franz. "I sent a message to the organ repairman in Salzburg. But I'm sure he will be too busy with the great organ in the cathedral to worry about our little organ. This will be a sad Christmas Eve for the people of St. Nicholas Church."

Franz said no more. Mrs. Gruber went back to her knitting.

Suddenly a knock at the door interrupted their silence.

Mrs. Gruber put aside her needles. Franz hurried to the door. There stood Father Joseph from St. Nicholas Church.

"*Grüss Gott.* God's Greeting," Franz said. Franz was pleased but surprised to see his friend out so late.

"*Grüss Gott*," said Father Joseph, greeting Franz in return.

Franz opened the door wider. "Come in. Come in," he said. "It is a cold night for such a long walk."

Father Joseph smiled as he entered the room. He nodded to Mrs. Gruber. "Good evening, Frau Gruber," he said.

He turned to Franz. "I am sorry to come so late, but something important happened. I couldn't wait." His breath came in short puffs from his walk up the valley.

Franz searched Father Joseph's face.

The priest came in and sat beside the fire. He warmed his hands in the halo of its heat. "I was preparing for the service. My thoughts filled with that first Christmas. Then a most mysterious thing happened! The words of a simple poem I wrote years ago suddenly came back to me."

Father Joseph took a piece of paper from his pocket and offered it to Franz. "Here, I have written down the words for you. Do you think you can find a melody in time for the Christmas Eve service?" He smiled. "Maybe we will have special music after all."

Franz shook his head. "No melody I write will take the place of Bach." Still, he took the paper from Father Joseph.

Much later, Franz sat at his desk. An empty sheet of music paper lay before him. Only the tick of the clock was there to keep him company. Over and over he squeezed his eyes shut trying to hear a melody. But there was nothing. "It is hopeless," he murmured.

Franz left his desk and went to the window. He gazed out into the night. Father Joseph's words echoed through his mind. *Silent night*, they said. *Holy night.*

Outside, the moon glided in and out of the clouds. Great shadows played hide-and-seek across the village roofs and over the snowy hills. The night was still.

All at once the organist's head filled with melody.

Quickly, he turned and picked up his pen. He dipped it into the pot of ink and began to write.

It was time for Franz Gruber to walk to St. Nicholas Church. Soon the Christmas Eve service would begin. He bundled up against the cold.

"Mama, I must go now," he said. He kissed his wife good-bye.

"We will follow in a little while," she replied.

"Papa, do you have your new song?" little Hans asked.

Franz patted his pocket and smiled at his young son.

"Papa, how will you make music without the organ?" asked Maria.

"You will see," Franz teased his daughter.

Franz found Father Joseph at the parish house next to the church. Father Joseph sat before his fire. The coals burned brightly in the grate.

"Ah, Father Joseph," Franz said. He unbuttoned his greatcoat. He reached into his pocket. "Here is your melody."

Father Joseph studied the music. A smile spread across his face. "It is as if the words and melody belong together."

Franz lowered his eyes. "I don't know where I found the melody," he said.

"Nor I the words," replied Father Joseph.

The bells rang in the church tower, calling everyone to the Christmas Eve service. Families came. Children led the way. "*Grüss Gott*," they called to each other. "And a blessed Christmas." Their lanterns twinkled across the mountainside.

With hushed voices, they entered the church.

Inside, the Christmas candles glowed. The children smiled at the beautiful sight. Mothers and fathers smiled, too. And they all took their seats.

"Where is the music?" someone asked.

Mrs. Gruber, Hans, and Maria sat in the front pew. Their eyes were bright with excitement. They had a secret.

Father Joseph stood high in the pulpit. "We will not hear the organ tonight," he said. "And we will miss it. Nevertheless, we will have music. For Franz Gruber and I have written a carol just for this night."

ather Joseph stepped from the pulpit. He picked up his guitar. Gently, he plucked the accompaniment. His high tenor voice began the melody. Franz joined in. His deep bass voice sang the harmony.

Silent Night, Holy Night

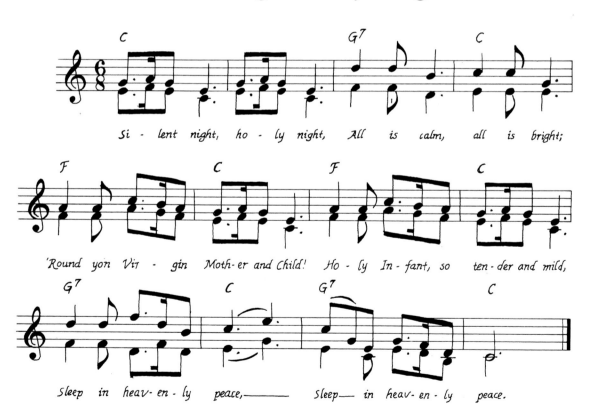

Si - lent night, ho - ly night, All is calm, all is bright;

'Round yon Vir - gin Moth - er and Child! Ho - ly In - fant, so ten - der and mild,

Sleep in heav - en - ly peace,——— Sleep—— in heav - en - ly peace.

The people listened. Soon they began to hum. Their hearts overflowed with joy. A light much greater than any candle filled the church.

Father Joseph nodded his approval. Franz beamed. Mrs. Gruber and the children clasped their hands in delight.

For they all understood. On that Christmas Eve, a carol was born.

Author's Note

Near the great Austrian city of Salzburg, there is a small town named Oberndorf. Here in 1818, a few days before Christmas, the organist of St. Nicholas Church discovered that the organ was damaged and would no longer play. The organist's name was Franz Gruber.

Using the words of Father Joseph Mohr, Franz Gruber quickly wrote the carol "Silent Night, Holy Night" to take the place of the organ music at the Christmas Eve service. It is said that the man who came to repair the organ heard the carol and took it back to Salzburg. Over time, "Silent Night, Holy Night" became popular, not only in Salzburg, but all over the world.

The story of how the carol was written was lost. For years it was thought to be a folk song with no known composer. Finally, in the early 1850s, when asked about the carol, Franz Gruber wrote to a friend and told him what had happened that Christmas in Oberndorf. From that time on, Franz Gruber and Father Joseph Mohr were given credit for writing the carol.

Today, St. Nicholas Church no longer stands in its original location along the Salzach River. Some years after the carol was written, the church was moved to higher ground to protect it from spring floods.

Still, if you go to Oberndorf, you will find a little chapel on that spot by the river. It stands there in memory of Franz Gruber, Father Joseph Mohr, and their beautiful carol.